W9-CKW-524

MATH
RiDDLES

A Viking Math Easy-to-Read

by Harriet Ziefert
illustrated by Andrea Baruffi

VIKING

VIKING
Published by the Penguin Group
Penguin Books USA Inc., 375 Hudson Street, New York, New York 10014, U.S.A.
Pénguin Books Ltd, 27 Wrights Lane, London W8 5TZ, England
Penguin Books Australia Ltd, Ringwood, Victoria, Australia
Penguin Books Canada Ltd, 10 Alcorn Avenue, Toronto, Ontario, Canada M4V 3B2
Penguin Books (N.Z.) Ltd, 182-190 Wairau Road, Auckland 10, New Zealand

Penguin Books Ltd, Registered Offices: Harmondsworth, Middlesex, England

First published in 1997 by Viking, a division of Penguin Books USA Inc.
Simultaneously published in Puffin Books

1   3   5   7   9   10   8   6   4   2

Text copyright © Harriet Ziefert, 1997
Illustrations copyright © Andrea Baruffi, 1997
All rights reserved

Library of Congress Catalog Card Number: 96-61641
ISBN 0-670-87498-1

Viking® and Easy-to-Read® are registered trademarks of Penguin Books USA Inc.

Printed in U.S.A.
Set in New Century Schoolbook

Reading Level 2.2

MATH

RiDDLES

A man had 12 sheep.
All but 9 died.
How many sheep did he have left?

He had 9 left.

Why is it dangerous to do

math in the jungle?

If you add 4 and 4, you get 8 (ate).

What has 18 legs and catches flies?

A baseball team.

Why is the moon like a dollar?

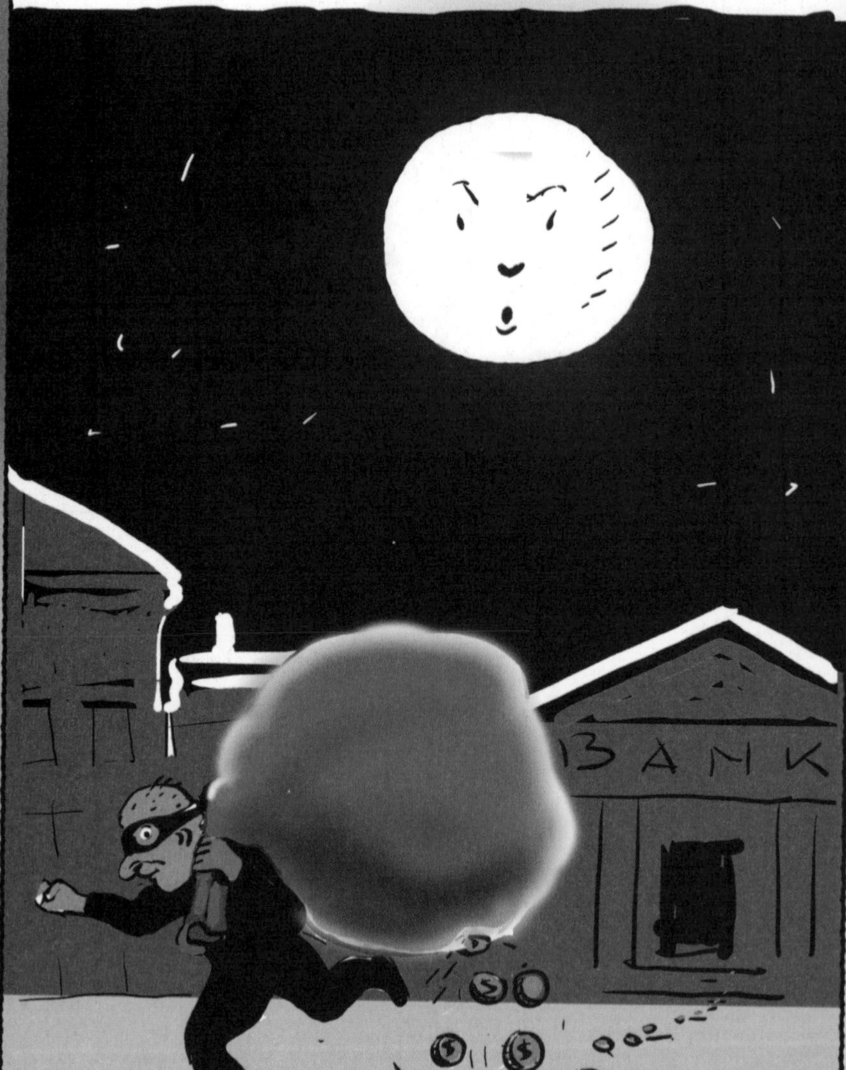

It has 4 quarters.

What is a bear cub after
it is 6 months old?

7 months old.

There were 99 penguins
on a boat.

The boat turned over.
How many were left?

There were 66 left.

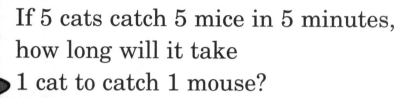

If 5 cats catch 5 mice in 5 minutes,
how long will it take
1 cat to catch 1 mouse?

5 minutes.

What is as big as an elephant,
but doesn't weigh anything?

An elephant's shadow.

Which weighs more—a pound of lead

or a pound of feathers?

They weigh the same.

If you have 5 potatoes
to divide equally among 3 pigs,
what should you do?

Mash them first.

How many worms make a foot?

12 inchworms.

What has 2 arms, 2 wings, 2 tails,

3 heads, 3 bodies, and 8 legs?

A man on horseback carrying a chicken.

If there were 9 cats in a boat
and 1 jumped out,
how many would be left?

None. They're copycats!

How many bugs can you put
in an empty bag?

1 bug. After that, the bag's not empty.

If you count 20 houses on your left going to school, and 20 on your right coming home,

how many different houses
have you counted?

20 houses. You counted the same
ones going and coming.

A frog fell into a well 6 feet deep. He could jump up 2 feet, but every time he did, he fell back 1 foot. How many times did he have to jump to get out of the well?

5. On the 5th jump, he was out.

What would you rather have,
a jar full of nickels or
half a jar full of dimes?

Either one. Each is worth the same.

On the way to a water hole
a zebra met 4 giraffes.
Each giraffe had 3 monkeys on its neck.

Each monkey had 2 birds on its tail.
How many animals were going to
the water hole?

1, the zebra. The others were coming back.

If you take 2 apples from 3 apples, how many do you have?

2 apples.

Why is the longest human nose
on record only 11 inches?

If it were any longer, it would be a foot.

MORE MATH FUN

- Math is about:

  counting things
  adding and subtracting
  comparing
  weighing and measuring
  shapes and sizes

  Go on a math riddle hunt.
  You can ask grown-ups if they know
  any riddles, or you can look in other
  riddle books.

- When you find a math riddle that
  you like, draw a picture to illustrate
  it. You may even want to draw two
  pictures: one to illustrate the
  question, and another to show
  the answer.

- How many people can you trick with
  the riddles from this book? After you
  fool them, can you explain the correct
  answers?